Cherish
Me

by
Joyce Carol Thomas
pictures by
Nneka Bennett

Joanna Cotler Books

HarperFestival

A Division of HarperCollinsPublishers

I sprang up from mother earth

She clothed me in her own colors

I was nourished by father sun

He glazed the pottery of my skin

I am beautiful by design

The pattern of night in my hair

The pattern of music in my rhythm

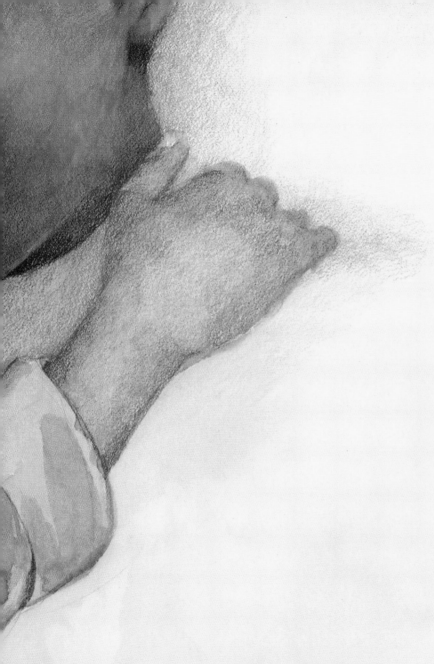

As you would cherish a thing of beauty

Cherish me

I sprang up from mother earth

    She clothed me in her own colors

I was nourished by father sun

    He glazed the pottery of my skin

I am beautiful by design

    The pattern of night in my hair

    The pattern of music in my rhythm

As you would cherish a thing of beauty

    Cherish me